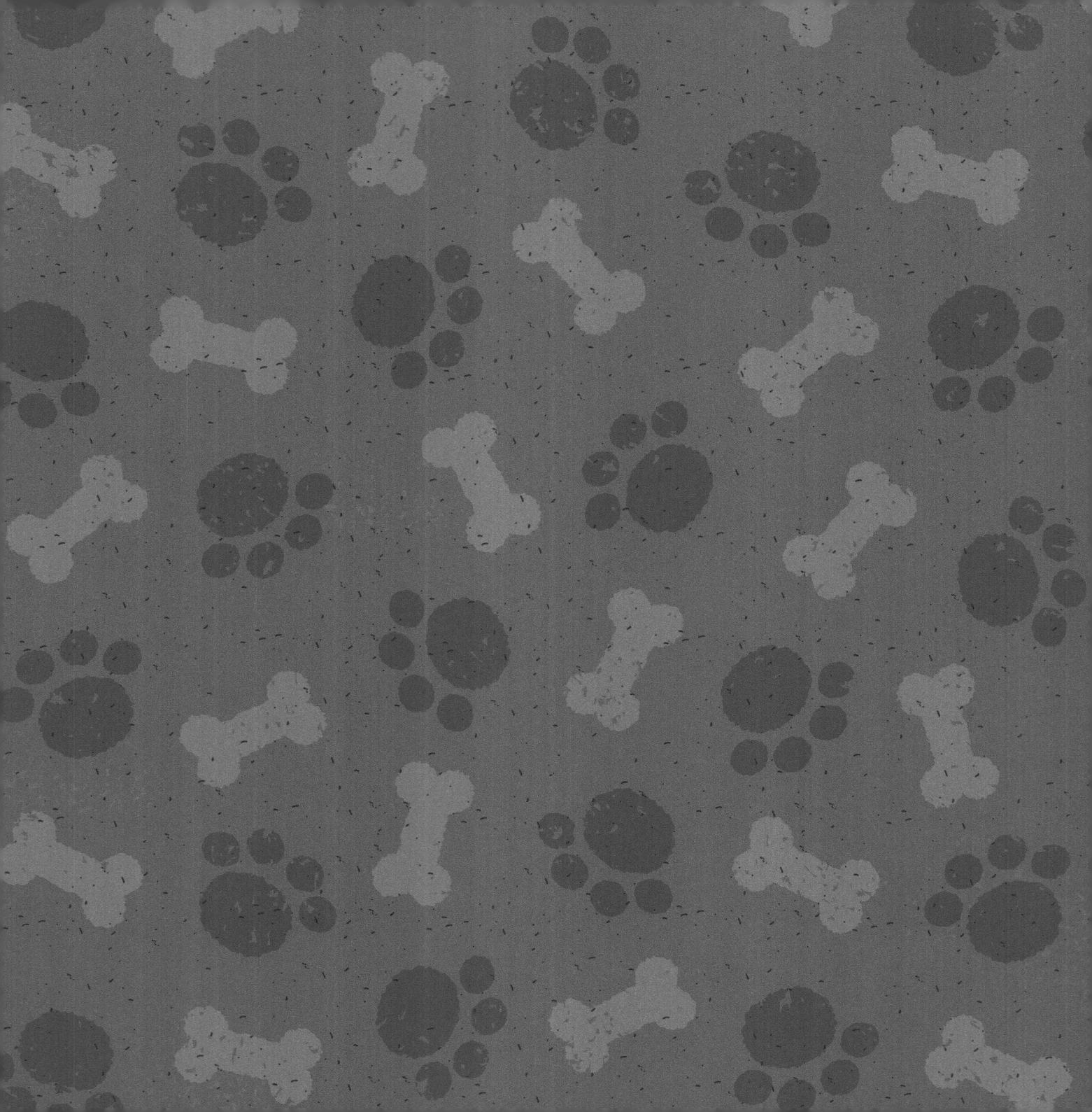

FOR PUP, POOCH, AND DOGGIE LOVERS EVERYWHERE.

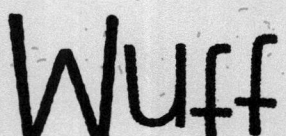

A part of Bright Ideas Graphics

Copyright © 2018 Mark C. Collins

All rights reserved. No part of this book may be reproduced or transmitted
in any form or by any means whatsoever without express written permission
from the author, except in the case of brief quotations embodied in critical articles and reviews.

This is Wuff.

RUFF

This is Wuff's stuff.

Wuff belongs to Duff.

Duff is buff!

Here is Duff's stuff.

Wuff and Duff play rough.

This is Puff.

Puff belongs to Duff.

This is Puff's stuff.

Puff naps on Wuff's fluff.

Wuff nabs Puff's scruff.

Wuff and Puff play rough.

Wuff is not so tough.

Wuff, Duff, and Puff live up on a bluff.

Next door lives Mr. Huff.

This is Huff's stuff.

Mr. Huff is rather gruff.

Duff gives Huff earmuffs.

Now Huff can't hear Wuff's ruffs!

Puff nabs Wuff's stuff.

Wuff grabs Duff's stuff.

RUFF

Wuff, Duff, and Puff play rough.

Wuff, Duff, Puff, and Huff have had enough.

The End

Bluff - A steep hill

Buff - Being in good physical shape

Fluff - An animal's fur

Gruff - Speaking in a short, angry way

Nab - To grab or take

Rough - Not orderly or smooth

Ruff - A dog's bark

Scruff - The back of an animal's neck

Stuff - A collection of things

Tough - Strong

Children's books are magical things!

As a child, I would lose myself in a good children's book, savoring each page in its illustrative glory. Often I took more time completing a book than necessary because I would study every illustration closely before proceeding to the next page. Now that I create my own children's books, I want to instill that same love and focus in young readers, that I had when I was a kid.
I hope you've enjoyed reading this book as much as I enjoyed creating it!

Mark Collins

Other books by Mark C. Collins
- Grandma Stinks!
- Ben's Day
- Meet The Bugs!
- Meet The Bugs! 2
- Harry's Hair
- The Christmas Cookies
- Witch Switch
- Where Did Summer Go?

Website: markcollinsillustration.com

- Mark Collins Illustration
- MCCollinsStudio
- MCCollinsStudio
- mccollinsstudio

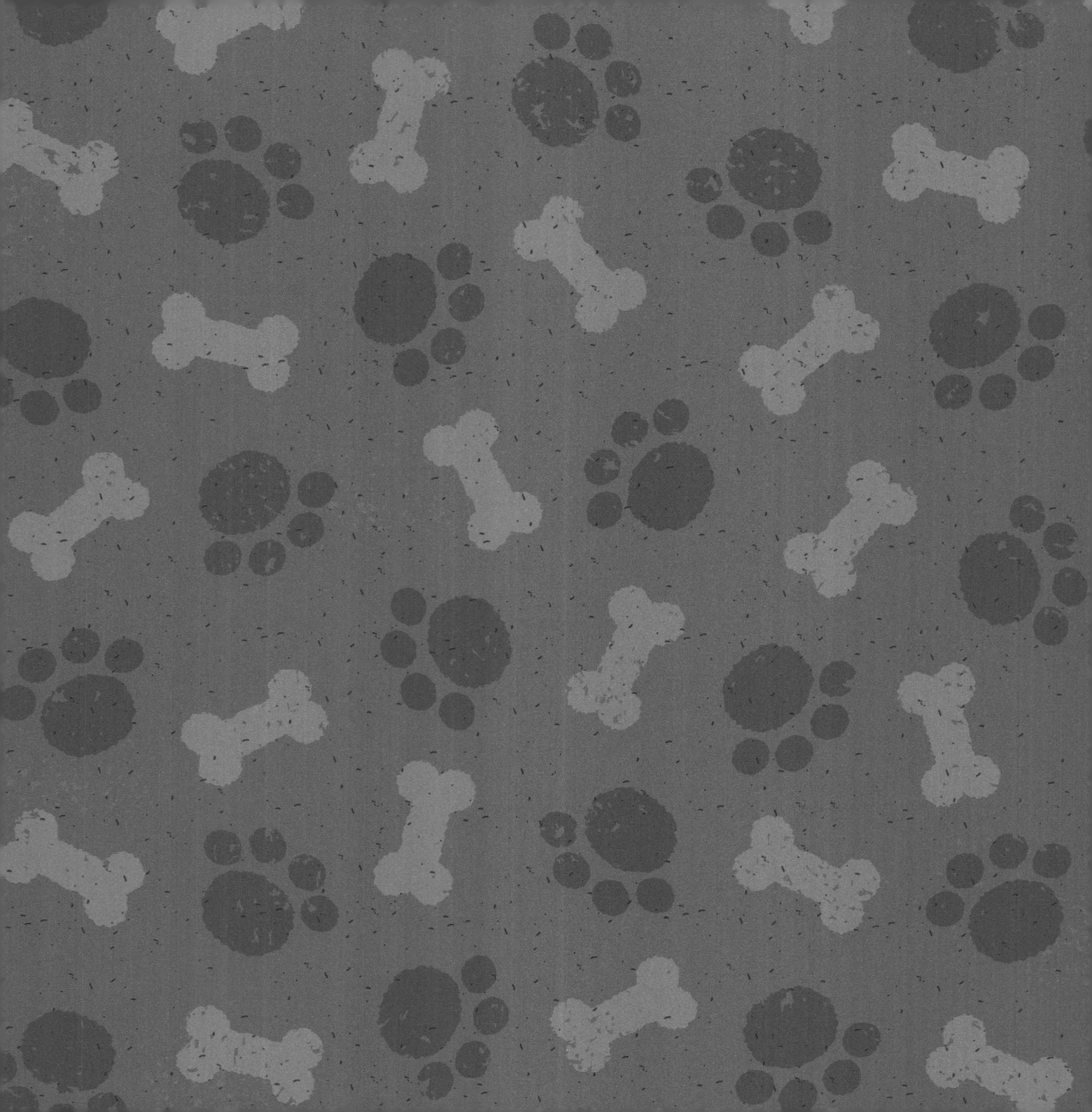

CPSIA information can be obtained
at www.ICGtesting.com
Printed in the USA
BVHW02n0342090718
521122BV00002B/9/P